AWESOME FACTS TO BLOW YOUR MIND

Illustrated by Skip Morrow

Written by Judith Freeman Clark & Stephen Long

A New England Publishing Associates Book

PRICE STERN SLOAN
Los Angeles

A New England Publishing Associates Book
Copyright © 1993 Price Stern Sloan, Inc.
Illustrations copyright © 1993 Skip Morrow.
Text copyright © 1993 Judith Freeman Clark, Stephen Long,
and New England Publishing Associates, Inc.

Published by Price Stern Sloan, Inc.,
A member of The Putnam & Grosset Group, New York, New York.

3 5 7 9 11 10 8 6 4 2

ISBN: 0-8431-3577-8

Library of Congress Catalog Number: 93-12252

Library of Congress Cataloging-in-Publication Data

Clark, Judith Freeman.
 Awesome Facts to blow your mind by Judith Freeman Clark;
illustrated by Skip Morrow.
     p. cm. — (Facts to blow your mind)
 Summary: Presents such interesting and bizarre facts as the
details of how spiders eat the insects they capture.
 ISBN 0-8431-3577-8
 1. Curiosities and wonders — Juvenile literature. (1. Curiosities
and wonders.) I. Morrow, Skip, Ill. II. Title. III. Series:
Clark, Judith Freemen, Facts to blow your mind.
AG243.C5636   1993
031.02 — dc20   93-12252
                                                   CIP
                                                   AC

Table of Contents

NATURAL WONDERS

As Smooth As Silk

Silk is a natural fiber. Unlike cotton, it doesn't come from a plant. Silk is made by a moth. A silkworm spins the fiber as it makes its cocoon. If the cocoon is left alone, it will hatch into a moth. But a silkworm cocoon can be unrolled like a spool of thread. When a single cocoon is unraveled, the result is more than 10 miles of silk thread!

I'll Take The Diet Special

Do you like to stuff yourself with burgers and fries at your local fast-food joint? Well, consider this: although it's one of the world's smallest mammals, the shrew has an appetite bigger than a human's. This tiny creature's body is only about 2 inches long, but it eats its own weight in food every day. To keep up with the shrew, a person weighing 100 pounds would need to eat more than 360 burgers and 20 orders of fries each day!

Dairy Farming, Ant-Style

Did you know that ants are farmers? They actually "herd" aphids—tiny bugs that drink plant sap. Ants keep herds of aphids together in small "barns" built of grass, and the aphids are let out of the barns to graze. From time to time, ants use their feelers to "milk" the aphids. They do this by stroking them so their bodies will ooze the sweet juice that ants love to drink.

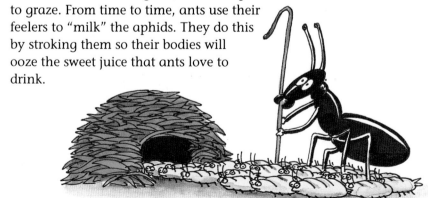

Waiting For A Rainy Day

If you've ever had a garden, you know how droopy plants can get after a week without any water. Imagine how the people of Calama, Chile felt when it rained one day in 1971— where no rain had fallen for 400 years!

No, Don't Show Me Pictures Of Your Grandchildren

Lemmings, which are small mammals, are capable of reproducing at a remarkable rate. One female lemming can have 12 babies in a single litter, and she may have three litters each season. A lemming can breed when it's only 19 days old—and give birth just three weeks later! That means one grandma lemming could have more than 1,000 grandchildren and 10,000 great-grandchildren.

A Whale Of A Creature

When kids get really mad, they sometimes stick out their tongues at people. Imagine an angry whale doing this. The Blue whale grows so big that its tongue weighs as much as an elephant!

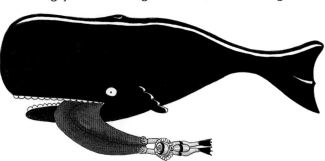

Just Use Some Sunscreen

If you watch plants growing indoors, you'll notice that they gradually grow toward the light. One plant—the redwood sorrel—actually turns away from light. When sunshine hits, it folds up its leaflets and shrinks downward, trying to hide. The redwood sorrel is so sensitive to light that its reaction begins 10 seconds after sunlight strikes and is complete in only six minutes.

I Smell A Rat

People often wonder why gigantic elephants seem to be afraid of tiny rats and mice. One good reason is that rats are fond of nibbling on elephant feet.

You're So Nosy

No two dogs have the same nose print. Like human fingerprints, an impression made from a dog's nose is unique.

The Better To See You With, My Dear

Each scallop, a shellfish popular among seafood-lovers, has 35 blue eyes that peer out from between the two halves of its shell.

You Eat Like A Bird

A hummingbird weighs a grand total of 3 grams. To maintain even this tiny weight, this most energetic of all warm-blooded creatures has to eat almost constantly. Every day, it eats half its weight in insect protein and sugar, and drinks eight times its weight in liquids. A 170-pound man with an equally hearty appetite would have to eat 155,000 calories a day. That's equal to about 285 pounds of hamburger!

A Bloody Lot

The blood in our body flows through an amazing network of blood vessels, including arteries, veins and the much smaller capillaries. The blood vessels in one person's body, if connected end to end, would encircle Earth more than two times. If you stacked your red blood cells one on top of another, you would create a tower 31,000 miles high!

Eggs-actly

The queen termite is an egg-laying machine—and a fast one at that. She squeezes out one egg per second! If you are good at multiplication, you know that this exceeds 3,000 eggs per hour, or more than 3 million termite eggs each year by one queen termite!

Get 'Em While They're Hot

Whales get too hot if they swim very fast. Especially in warmer ocean waters, near the equator, whales have been known to die because they were unable to cool themselves off. When whalers kill one of these enormous beasts, they immediately slit it open so that water can pour through the belly and cool down the carcass. Whales must be processed quickly or heat from the whale's decaying body will actually burn up its bones.

Do We Have Enough Flashlight Batteries?

In March 1989, a storm cut off electrical power for nine hours to 6 million people in and around Montreal, Canada. It wasn't a snowstorm or a hurricane. It was a solar storm. Bursts of solar energy spark tremendous electrical charges when they strike Earth's magnetic field, sometimes causing blackouts like Montreal's. Solar storm activity tends to follow 22-year cycles. We entered a three-year period of peak activity in 1992.

A Nose By Any Other Name

The human nose does a lot of work. It takes in an average of 12 to 15 breaths per minute—around 20,000 each day or 7 million a year. Each breath contains an average of 500 cubic centimeters of air —or about the amount it takes to pump up a football. That means the nose breathes in enough air every day to fill about 5,000 birthday balloons. This is a big job for a small chunk of skin and cartilage, but the nose does have a system for resting. The nostrils work in shifts. Each nostril does the breathing for two to four hours, while the other one...takes a breather.

Not Too Hot, Not Too Cold

A polar bear's body is designed in such a way so that it can stay warm when it is as cold as -49° Fahrenheit, or when air temperature is much higher. Under its fur, the bear has a layer of blubber more than 4 inches thick to help it keep warm. When its body gets too hot, a polar bear pants to fill its lungs with cold air, and its heartbeat increases from 45 to 148 beats per minute. Mother polar bears hibernating in winter with their cubs sometimes lose about 400 pounds of excess blubber, because they live on the stored-up fat while nursing.

World's Oldest Plant

Although humans cannot watch Tyrannosaurus rex stride through a forest, or watch a 5-ton Brontosaurus lumber slowly by, one species of plant has survived unchanged from the era of the dinosaurs and still grows on Earth, just as it did 200 million years ago. Ginkgoaceae, or the Ginkgo tree, is the single plant to have survived and prospered from prehistoric times to the present. The Ginkgo can be seen today, flourishing in many gardens and parks throughout Europe and North America, as well as in Japan and China— truly a living dinosaur!

Gone Fishing

If you've ever dug earthworms for fishing, you probably remember how pleased you were when you found an extra-fat specimen. Imagine how satisfying it would be to dig for earthworms in Australia, where giant earthworms have been known to grow to a length of 11 feet! These enormous creatures can weigh in at nearly 2 pounds and one would provide plenty of bait for fishing—but they are considered so rare they are protected by laws from being dug up.

Are You Worth Your Weight In Ants?

If you have ever seen an ant pulling a dead bee or butterfly along, you may have wondered how such a small insect can be so strong. Ants are capable of moving things much bigger and heavier than themselves, and scientists have often wondered how this is possible. Some scientists have calculated that if an ant were the same size as a human being, it would be able to move 240,000 pounds!

He's Got Rhythm!

How do crickets make their characteristic chirping noise? The talent is confined to the male cricket, which has ribbed "teeth" on the side of its body. He rubs his wings rhythmically along the teeth—5,000 times per second! The chirping song that results can be heard up to a mile away.

All Aflutter

Hummingbirds flap their tiny wings about 55 times per second. When they are mating, their wings flutter as fast as 200 times per second.

High-Flying

The common dragonfly is one of the world's fastest-flying insects. It is able to zip around at speeds of up to 60 miles per hour! And although dragonflies are only a few inches across today, some varieties that are now extinct had wingspreads of nearly 3 feet!

The Great-grandfather Of All Plants

Probably the oldest living organism in the world was discovered recently in Michigan. It might also be the largest living thing on Earth. A giant fungus, estimated to be 10,000 years old, was found growing in the ground there. Scientists think that the fungus weighs about 100 tons—about as much as a Blue whale—and when they measured it, it covered 30 acres of land near Crystal Falls, Michigan.

You Have To Baby-sit Tonight

An Emperor penguin mother lays just one egg at the beginning of winter, but it's the father penguin who huddles over the egg and keeps it warm. The mother goes in search of food, staying away for about two months, while Dad hatches the egg alone. Since the egg would freeze if he left to get food, he survives only on the fat stored in his body. By the time Mom returns to feed and care for their baby, Dad—skinny as a rail—has lost 33 percent of his body weight!

There's Fire Down Below

Oceanographers recently discovered the world's largest group of active volcanoes in the South Pacific near the Easter Islands. Using special sonar equipment, scientists found 1,133 underwater volcanoes covering the ocean floor in a space nearly the size of New York state. Some of these volcanoes are almost 7,000 feet high, but the ocean is so deep the tops of the cones remain hidden 2,500 feet or more below the water's surface.

MIND-NUMBING NUMBERS

What Eon Is It?

A thousand years ago, some people in Europe feared the world would end in the year 1000. Even today a few people believe the end is near because we're approaching the year 2000. One of the many reasons not to worry too much is that in many countries it's a different year altogether! According to the Japanese calendar, it will be the year 2660, and it will be 5761 on the Jewish calendar. For Babylonians it would be the year 2749—and it is 7509 if you count according to a calendar used during the Byzantine Era.

The World's Biggest Sleepover

About 2 million microscopic dust mites can be found in the mattress, blankets and pillows of an average double bed. This tiny animal lives in houses everywhere. It exists completely on a diet of human skin flakes. These skin flakes fall from our bodies naturally during the course of the day. They drift to the floor or to furniture cushions and similar surfaces. As a result, the dust mite thrives on the never-ending banquet we set for it everywhere.

Did We Forget Anything?

Does your family's grocery-shopping list seem long? Imagine having to shop for the food used by an international airline. A big airline employs hundreds of food-service workers to prepare about 200,000 meals every week. All this cooking means the airline must buy huge amounts of everything. For example, one airline shopping list for the week included about 30,000 chickens, 8,000 heads of lettuce and almost 200,000 tomatoes!

I've Lost Count

Bugs are extremely common in many parts of the world. In South America, scientists have counted as many as 40,000 insect species in only 2 1/2 acres of rain forest. Scientists studying bugs in Panama have found 950 different species of beetles in only one species of tree.

Room For One More

The Mediterranean country of Monaco is the most densely populated nation in the world. In 1992, its population density was 49,520 people per square mile! By contrast, China—with more than 1 billion people—has only 409 people per square mile. The entire nation of Monaco covers little more than half a square mile, but there are 29,712 people living there.

Mooooo - urp!

Burping in public is bad manners, but at least it's not harmful to the environment. Cows, on the other hand, belch twice a minute and each time they do they release methane, one of the gases that heat up Earth's atmosphere. Cows expel as much as one-half pound of methane each day. Since there are 1.3 billion heads of cattle in the world, they add close to 100 million tons of methane to the atmosphere each year.

A Close Shave

An important milestone for most teenage boys is their first shave. No matter how careful they are, most have a bit of trouble learning to use a razor. But after a while, shaving becomes easy or routine, which isn't surprising since it has to be done every day. A man's beard grows quickly. Every 24 hours up to 25,000 hairs of 0.5 millimeter (about one-fiftieth of an inch) in length reappear on a man's face!

Slow Down, You're Moving Too Fast!

Before their parachutes open, free-falling skydivers regularly find themselves plummeting 185 miles per hour through the air. The fastest speed recorded by a skydiver was 614 m.p.h.

Hair-Raising Work

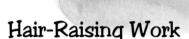

Some researchers have determined that a single human hair can support two or three ounces in weight. On an average young man's head, there are 110,000 strands of hair. This means that one head of hair could hold up a weight of more than 5,000 pounds—about what a full-size pickup truck weighs!

Home, Sweet Home!

You may not realize it, but the human body is a big place. An average man has about 20 square feet of skin! That's as big as a 4' x 5' piece of carpet. His skin's surface is so roomy that it's home to billions of mites and bacteria. More microscopic organisms live on humans than on any other creature. In fact, there are more tiny creatures living on your skin than people living on Earth!

Here Today, Gone Tomorrow

Although there are an estimated 10 million species of animals and plants living on Earth today, extinction threatens many of them. In fact, many scientists fear that, by the year 2000, environmental damage and the thoughtless behavior of humans could result in the total destruc-tion of 20 per-cent of these existing species. This means that 3 million types of plants and animals could disappear for-ever in just a few short years.

Oh, Rats!

People don't like rats because they are scavengers—and because they can cause sicknesses like typhoid, and the dreaded bubonic plague. Even more frightening, however, is the impact of the rat population—estimated to be 125 million in the United States alone—on human food supplies. One rat can devour 40 pounds of food annually. That means the entire rat population destroys one-fifth of all Earth's grain crops each year.

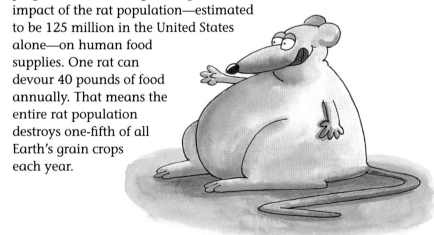

Guzundheit!

You've probably noticed how violently the air leaves your nose and mouth as you sneeze, but have you ever clocked the speed? Researchers say sneezing blasts air from your body at 85 percent of the speed of sound, or about 630 miles per hour.

Lay Off Our Feathered Friends!

A ceremonial cape worn by Hawaiian King Kamehameha was made from the yellow feathers of the 'o'o-'a'a bird, which is now almost extinct; only one is left in the entire world. It's easy to understand why. The king's cape was made of feathers taken from 80,000 birds.

Into The Deep, Blue Sea

The Amazon is the largest and most powerful river in the world. It carries 3 billion gallons of water each day—20 percent of the world's flowing water. It is so powerful that it runs as a freshwater river 200 miles out into the salt water of the Atlantic Ocean!

Busy Body

Wonder why you're so tired at night? Every day, about 2 billion cells die in the human body—but are immediately replaced. There are more than 600 major muscles in the human body, along with 206 bones. A person blinks about 25 times each minute, the salivary glands produce nearly two quarts of saliva in 24 hours, and a person's heart will pump 46 million gallons of blood during his or her lifetime —enough to fill about 3,000 backyard swimming pools!

An Eskimo Light Show

The aurora borealis, or northern lights, puts on an unpredictable but spectacular show. Often looking like a huge, shimmering curtain of colored light, it can be several hundred miles long and 150 miles high. Scientists believe that "sun storms" cause the northern lights, and that they follow an 11-year cycle. It occurs over the North Magnetic Pole, from an electrical charge containing a current of 1 trillion watts. That's enough electrical power to light about 15 100-watt light bulbs in every home in the United States.

Right On Target

In 1415, at the battle of Agincourt, the English King Henry V had an army of archers skilled in the use of the recently invented longbow. They destroyed the French army in just 30 minutes, killing 25,000 French soldiers while losing only 500 of their own. The secret was the archers' ability with the new weapon. A really good English bowman could fire seven steel-pointed arrows each minute, each arrow going about 400 feet.

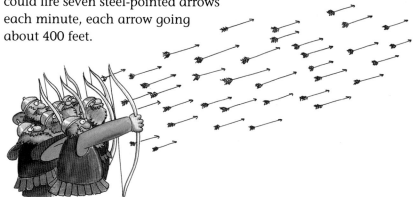

BIG JOBS

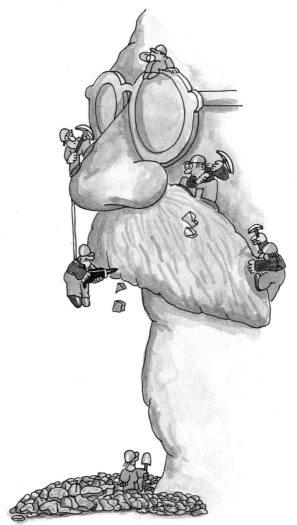

Modeling Clay Would Have Been Easier

Have you seen pictures of the giant faces of U.S. Presidents George Washington, Thomas Jefferson, Abraham Lincoln, and Theodore Roosevelt carved into Mount Rushmore in the Black Hills of South Dakota? They took nearly 400 men a total of 14 years to complete. By the time they finished the project in 1941, workers had carried away 450,000 tons of granite.

Heavy Art

Ancient people all over the world performed feats of construction that seem impossible when you think about the crude tools they used. On Easter Island in the southern Pacific Ocean, enormous statues were carved and put in place along the island coastline. Scientists agree that the largest of these statues weighs about 80 tons! It was probably made at a stone quarry by several dozen craftsmen, then moved into place by a team of nearly 100 men who used ropes to pull the heavy load. Scientists figure that it may have taken nearly six months to move one statue and put it in a standing position!

Have You Seen The Doors?

Lorenzo Ghiberti (1378-1455), an Italian sculptor, lived in Florence and spent 48 years making a single pair of doors for a church in his city. Made of bronze, they illustrated scenes from the Old Testament. When the doors were finished, they were so beautiful that the great artist Michelangelo called them the "gates of paradise."

Looking For A Job?

It can take several hundred workers up to two or three years to build a skyscraping office building. During the time of the Egyptian pharaohs, the number of workers needed to build the 10 pyramids at Giza was somewhere around 100,000! Not only that, it took these workers longer than 20 years to complete the structures, one of which is 48 stories tall!

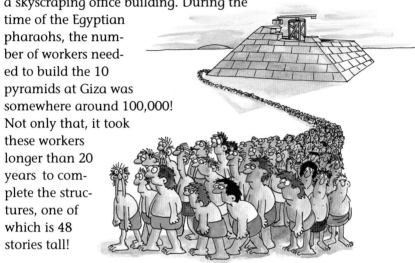

What Are You Complaining About?

Do you complain when your parents ask you to help out around the house? Do you gripe when they ask you to empty the trash or make your bed? If you had lived 2,200 years ago, you might have had to help build the Great Wall of China. About 300,000 Chinese soldiers were in charge of the work. They forced another million people—including kids—to do the actual building! No one had any choice about it, and people had to work summer and winter. They often had little food or water. Most parts of the Great Wall still standing now were built about 500 years ago. If the entire wall were in place, it would stretch nearly 4,000 miles across China!

I Don't Understand A Single Word You've Said

During World War II, the U.S. Army tried to develop ways to transmit radio messages that the enemy could not understand. The most successful was not even a secret code. It was the Navajo Indian language. Native Americans from Arizona and New Mexico became "code talkers," translating the Army's messages into Navajo and sending the information by radio to another code talker. Nobody else knew what they were saying and all enemy attempts to break the code ended in failure.

A Hot Spot To Be In

In dry, drought-ridden areas, forest fires can spread quickly. Sometimes the flames move as fast as 90 miles per hour! Next time you're traveling along the highway, look at your car's speedometer. Imagine how much faster a forest fire can move, and what a big job it is to control one.

In one California fire several years ago, as many as 4,500 firefighters using 376 fire trucks and water tankers were pressed into service during a single night. Ninety-four bulldozers were used to clear open areas called "firebreaks" of everything that could burn to stop the fire from spreading. And 13 air tankers bombed the area with thousands of gallons of water in hopes of dousing the flames.

Highly Regarded Art

In the 1920s, a series of lines carved into desert sand in Peru baffled scientists. There was no explanation for the lines nor any way to figure out how they had been made. The evidence showed, however, that the lines had been drawn in the desert

more than 2,000 years earlier. In 1941, Peruvian pilots took photographs of these lines, which they found covered several hundred square miles of desert sand. The photos seemed to show a monkey drawing, and other pictures, recognizable only from the air! To this day, nobody knows how or why ancient artists made the huge drawings that can only be admired from an airplane.

A Real Cool Job

Until electricity was widely available, ice was considered a luxury item. During the late 1890s, people tried different ways of bringing ice to regions where there were no refrigerators. One experiment in ice-hauling led a group of explorers to the Antarctic. There, they put masts and sails on small icebergs and floated with them to Peru—more than 2,000 miles away!

Pass The Pretzels

In the Amazon region of South America, some natives drink lots of beer. Because beer is brewed only by women, men often have several wives to make sure they don't run out of home brew. Everyone in the tribe drinks—including women and children—but men swig down the most. Each hunter consumes three or four gallons of beer each day, or the equivalent of five to seven six-packs.

I Don't Love You That Much

In love songs, people pledge to climb the highest mountain or swim the deepest ocean. If they actually did that, they would have to start with a trip to Nepal so they could climb Mount Everest, which soars 29,028 feet into the air. Swimming the deepest sea, the Pacific Ocean, would be much more difficult. Its average depth is 12,925 feet, or more than two miles, and its deepest spot is the Mariana Trench, which plunges down to 35,840 feet. Swimming the Pacific from Panama to Asia would cover 11,000 miles, a real test of true love!

A Taxing Idea

In colonial America, squirrels were numerous and troublesome, eating food stored up for livestock and people. Some colonial governments offered bounty money in exchange for dead squirrels, just as they offered bounty for dead outlaws! In 1749 in Pennsylvania alone, 640,000 squirrels were turned in for bounty money. In Ohio, colonists once were able to pay taxes in dead squirrels instead of money!

Bloody Work

Buffalo Bill Cody, a Wild West scout and hunter, was hired by the railroads in the late 1860s to kill bison. Shot for meat to feed railroad workers and passengers, they also were killed because the herds stampeded by the millions across new railroad tracks. In just 18 months, Buffalo Bill single-handedly shot 4,000 bison. Working with other hunters, he led a ruthless war against these enormous, woolly beasts. By the early 1870s, 2.5 million bison had been killed. By the end of the century, fewer than 1,000 bison remained out of the original herds of 30 or 40 million!

The Great Stone Mystery

You may have learned in school about the ancient Incas. They lived in the Andes mountains of South America. They are famous for having built great cities without using any machinery. Although most of these cities fell into ruins hundreds of years ago, one that still stands is a giant fortress of stone near what is now Cuzco, Peru. The men who built the fortress had no power tools or machines for cutting or hauling stone, and their construction methods remain a mystery. Archaeologists believe the stones, many weighing at least 100 tons, were moved from rock quarries many miles away from the fortress location. No one knows how, because it would take at least 2,000 people to haul each stone and lift it into place in the fortress wall!

A Hard Day's Work

How would you spend a billion dollars? Spending $1,000 each day for 75 years wouldn't even make a dent in it. You would have to spend $36,529—about the cost of a luxury car—each day for 75 years to spend a billion dollars. Of course, if you put the money in a savings account, the interest it earned would grow much faster than you could spend it. In fact, just to stay even, you would have to spend more than $100,000 every day.

STAGGERING WEIGHTS & MEASURES

Time For A Change

Americans throw away nearly 20 million disposable diapers each year—enough to fill up one huge garbage barge every six hours. A single baby uses almost $2,000 worth of disposable diapers before graduating to regular underwear.

For That Hard-To-Reach Itch

Do you bite your fingernails? It's one way of making sure that they stay short! Some people go to great lengths not to have short nails. In 1952 a man in India stopped cutting his fingernails. By being very careful, he was able to avoid breaking them. Thirty-seven years later the thumb nail on the man's left hand had grown to a length of 39 inches!

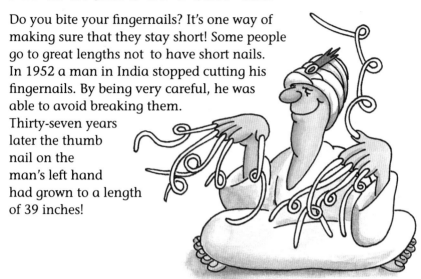

Burn Those Calories Off!

The world's fattest person weighed almost 1,200 pounds. In 1987 he got stuck trying to walk through his bedroom doorway. To help free him from this uncomfortable position, the fire department was called. It took nearly a dozen firemen to help get the man unstuck and back to his bedroom, where he spent almost all of his time.

Just Like Camping

During the Ice Age, when tools and building materials were scarce, people sometimes built shelters out of mammoth bones. Archaeologists have discovered that these crude houses, in which huge tusks, skulls, and jawbones were the "building blocks," weighed as much as 46,000 pounds!

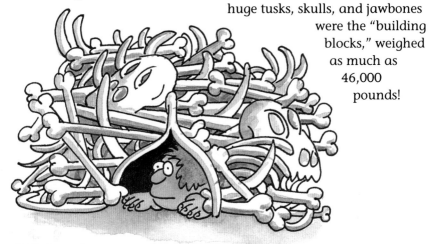

We're Outnumbered

Did you ever wonder how many insects there are? Well, nobody has counted them, but scientists figure that for every person alive there are 12 times that person's weight in insects buzzing and crawling and flying around. In fact, scientists say there are about a ton of termites for each person on Earth!

Eat Up, You're A Growing Boy!

A normal rate of weight gain for growing cows is 1.5 pounds per day. This may not seem like much but if you were a calf and gained the normal rate each day, you might weigh 60 pounds when you began fourth grade —and almost 500 pounds at the start of summer vacation!

How Many Birthdays Is That?

The Hubble Space Telescope has been sending information back to Earth telling us that there is nothing in outer space to stop the universe from expanding. This means that the universe will continue to grow. However, from the telescope's data scientists estimate the universe is already pretty old. Most think it has been around for 15 billion years!

MIRACLES OF SCIENCE

Going Up!

You know the stomach-jolting sensation caused by a ride in an elevator? It feels like you're leaving your insides far behind as you travel very quickly up or down inside a building. Some elevators travel at very high speeds. In Chicago's Sears Tower, the elevators go as fast as 300 feet per second.

Bag It

Scientists have discovered that if you put an apple in a paper bag it will get red faster than if you leave the fruit to ripen in the sun. The reason is that ethylene gas—produced by the fruit—stimulates the ripening process. Researchers also discovered that a paper bag especially helps the apple get ripe because it lets in oxygen, another gas necessary for ripening. If you put an apple in a plastic bag, the oxygen is shut out. This is why fruit in supermarkets is often packaged in plastic to keep it from ripening too fast and spoiling.

Bridge To Nowhere?

The longest bridge in the world is in Louisiana. It is the Lake Ponchartrain Bridge #2, which is nearly 24 miles long! When you ride across it, you come to an eight-mile stretch where you can't see land on either side.

Dr. Jones, Please Pass The Fudge Ripple

Scientists spend a lot of time working on really important things like cures for cancer and new forms of energy. Lucky for us, they also spend time on other projects, like improving ice cream. Scientists have now produced a protein that copies a substance found in flounder, a fish that lives on the ocean floor, where it's pretty cold. The protein acts like antifreeze and extends the life of ice cream and other frozen foods.

Light Up My Life

An ordinary light bulb glows when a tiny thread of tungsten wire gets white-hot because of the electricity flowing through it. Because the wire is so fine and sensitive, it doesn't last long. An average light bulb lasts about six months if it's left on for four hours each day. Scientists have developed a new light bulb that lasts much longer because it doesn't contain wires—instead, it works on high-frequency radio waves and can last up to 14 years!

BREAK OPEN THE PIGGY BANK

A Costly Project

You may have heard that the minerals and other elements in your body would cost several dollars if you were to buy them at a chemical supply store. But the cost of assembling these raw materials into a human being would cost a bit more. According to one study, it would take about $6 million in hormones and other substances, plus several trillion dollars more to develop the technology to make these substances into human cells. (That is three times what the U.S government spends each year.) And these calculations don't include the cost of putting these cells together into a human form!

Recycle That Sheep

Does your family recycle bulk paper items such as newspapers? Many people do, but few pay much attention to how much writing paper we toss in the trash each day. Paper is so cheap that we often throw away more than we actually use. Paper didn't even exist 2,000 years ago. Writing was done then on parchment made from the skin of goats or sheep. Parchment was very expensive to produce. That's why it was almost never thrown away. To make a 200-page book out of parchment required the skins of as many as a dozen sheep!

Everything's Rosey

First-century Roman Emperor Nero made rose water and rose petals fashionable. During one dinner, he ordered his servants to scatter rose perfume, blossoms and other rose-scented material around the banquet rooms. The cost of scent for this single event was equal to $160,000 in today's money.

How About A Superman Comic Book?

People are willing to spend a lot of money for something that's really special. Imagine spending millions of dollars for one book. In 1987, a rare, 15th-century copy of the famed Gutenburg Bible, named after and printed by the inventor of movable type, sold at a New York City auction for more than $5 million!

All That Glitters

The opening of King Tutankhamen's tomb in 1923 made people gasp in disbelief when they learned about the young king's coffin. It was made of solid gold and weighed 243 pounds! If you go to Cairo, Egypt, you can see the gold coffin on display at a museum there. It is priceless because it's a unique piece of art. If the container for the king's body were melted down to gold bars, the gold alone would be worth almost $1.3 million.

PHENOMENAL PEOPLE

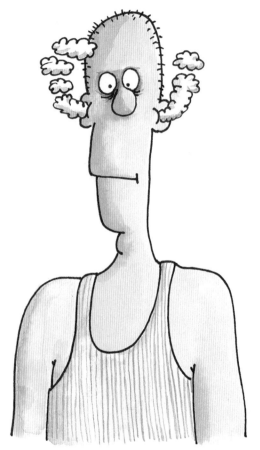

Seven Strikes And You're Out!

Who says lightning doesn't strike twice in the same place? One park ranger in Virginia was hit by lightning seven times between 1942 and 1977! He lost his hair, his eyebrows got burned off, and his arms and legs were badly burned. It's hard to believe he survived even one strike. A bolt of lightning travels up to 1,000 miles per second and is six times hotter than the surface of the sun!

Directory Assistance

Some people are blessed with a "photographic memory." A 7-year-old girl named Harriet was one such remarkable person. One day, her father read her the first three pages of the phone book. For several years afterward, she could recall the names and numbers of everyone on those pages!

Thanks, I'll Just Have Water

Harry Houdini dazzled audiences with his ability to escape from handcuffs, straitjackets and prison cells. Once, he escaped from a large, padlocked milk can totally filled with water, into which he was placed in handcuffs. Houdini could make successful underwater escapes because he was able to hold his breath for a long time. However, he was almost killed when he accepted a British brewer's challenge to escape from a full beer barrel. Houdini, a non-drinker, fell unconscious because of the alcoholic fumes and had to be rescued from the barrel by his assistant.

The Better To See You With

A telescope or pair of binoculars helps if you want to see faraway things more easily. But a Frenchman living more than a century ago in an African colony didn't need them. Supposedly, he had such strong eyesight that he could see up to 600 miles away —without glasses or other lenses! By seeing "atmospheric disturbances" on the horizon, he correctly predicted the arrival of sailing ships. Sometimes he could "see" the ships up to four days before anyone else!

Hit Me With Your Best Shot

During the early 1900s Russia's "mad monk" Rasputin was popular with the Czar, but he had many enemies at the court who wanted to kill him. One winter night, these plotters invited Rasputin for dinner and fed him cakes and wine filled with cyanide. None of the poison affected Rasputin. He just talked, joked and enjoyed the wine. In desperation, one of the plotters shot him at point-blank range. Instead of keeling over dead, the powerful monk jumped up and grabbed his attackers —who shot him again and again until he lay still. They then dumped him in a river. Days later he was found, dead at last, a victim of drowning!

Hold It!

A trucker named Bob LaGree pulled into a rest stop along a New York highway one October night in 1985 and parked his 18-wheeler. Starting to walk across the parking area, LaGree saw another truck suddenly slide toward him, pinning him against his own truck. LaGree, a fomer professional wrestler, tried to push the two rigs apart and get free but

couldn't do it until another man came along. Together, they managed to push apart the two 31-ton rigs enough for LaGree to slip out before he was squashed like a pancake. LaGree just limps a little as a result of his encounter with the runaway truck.

A Barrel Of Fun

In 1901, a woman named Anna Taylor rode over Niagara Falls inside a wooden barrel! Sealed in the barrel, she was carried over the 158-foot-high falls in a raging surge of pounding water. It took three seconds for the barrel to complete its tumbling drop, and then

another 10 seconds for the barrel to pop to the surface of the water after it went over the falls. When the container was pulled from the water, Anna Taylor climbed out, bruised but generally unhurt. She earned money by traveling all around the United States lecturing about her exploit. One observer said Taylor got a lot of credit that "should have gone to the barrel."

The Human Fly

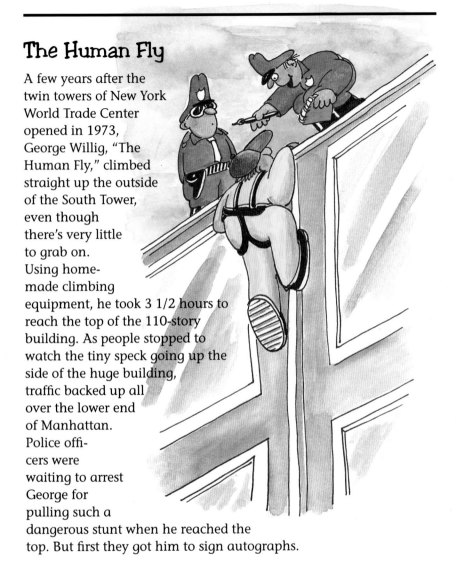

A few years after the twin towers of New York World Trade Center opened in 1973, George Willig, "The Human Fly," climbed straight up the outside of the South Tower, even though there's very little to grab on. Using home-made climbing equipment, he took 3 1/2 hours to reach the top of the 110-story building. As people stopped to watch the tiny speck going up the side of the huge building, traffic backed up all over the lower end of Manhattan. Police officers were waiting to arrest George for pulling such a dangerous stunt when he reached the top. But first they got him to sign autographs.